Gordon
goes too fast

Illustrated by Robin Davies
Series Editor: Teresa Wilson

All rights reserved
Published in Great Britain in 2002 by Egmont Books Limited,
239 Kensington High Street, London, W8 6SA
Printed in Italy
ISBN 0 7498 5484 7

10 9 8 7 6 5 4 3 2 1

Educational consultant: Betty Root, formerly Director of the Reading Centre in the University of Reading.

Henry was happy as he pulled the coaches.

When he looked up he saw the birds in their nests.

It was very quiet.

The birds flapped their wings
at Henry and the coaches.

One day, Henry was sick.

The Fat Controller asked Gordon to pull the coaches for Henry.

"I will," said Gordon.

He wanted to show the coaches
how fast he could go.

The coaches didn't like going fast.

"Please slow down," they said.

"I won't," said Gordon.

The birds didn't like Gordon going fast.

The smoke from his funnel frightened them.

They wanted him to slow down.

The next day Gordon frightened them again.

The coaches were very cross.

They liked Henry to pull them.

The coaches said to The Fat Controller,
"Gordon was going too fast.
He frightened the birds."

The Fat Controller was cross.

The next day, Gordon tried
to pull the coaches.

They would not move.

He pulled and pulled,
but they would not move.

There were too many coaches.

19

Henry came up. "Hello," he said.

Gordon was very cross.

"You can pull your own coaches," he said.

They all laughed as Gordon hurried away.

The Fat Controller took some of the coaches away.

Henry was ready to go.

The birds flew down and flapped their wings.

They were happy it was quiet again.